Atlantic City's Most Wanted #1

Charity Parkerson

Punk & Sissy Publications

Copyright

CHARITY PARKERSON

Editor: BZ Hercules & Consultants

Photographer: CJC Photography

Models: Kevin R. Davis

Brandon English

CONTENTS

Introduction	1
Author Note	3
Chapter One	4
Chapter Two	17
Chapter Three	25
Chapter Four	39
Chapter Five	51
Chapter Six	62
Chapter Seven	74
Chapter Eight	95

Chapter Nine   114

Chapter Ten   125

Chapter Eleven   141

About the Author   146

Introduction

Two men on opposite sides of the law. *Neither one cares.*

Gable has spent years with the FBI. He's a liaison between his department and the CIA. It's a nice gig that allows him a lot of freedom. It's also a position that's put him in the company of more than a few shady men. Cutler may not top that list, but he's definitely the one who has Gable's attention. Now Gable is ready for a change of scenery. His new location and position with the CIA lands him practically full time in the path of the hottest criminal he's ever met. It's a race to see which of them falls first.

Cutler didn't earn his place in the world through hard work and dedication. His wealth was handed to him for being willing to do whatever it took for a not-so-clean organization. Luckily, it's the kind of money that also shields him from the law. Unfortunately, or fortunately, depending on how one looks at things, it's not keeping him safe from one very delicious CIA agent. He's in real danger of getting locked down, but not in the way he always expected.

Ruined is the first book in Charity Parkerson's Atlantic City's Most Wanted series. These are sexy and sometimes dark stories where the richest and most dangerous men in Atlantic City meet their match. These are best enjoyed when read in order.

Author Note

This is a dark romance series, including murder, abuse, drug use, and crime lords. If you haven't read the prequel, Captivated, you might want to start there. Thanks for reading!

CHAPTER ONE

THERE WASN'T A SINGLE charity event hosted by Zander Kapra—the man who ran Vegas—or his people that Cutler didn't attend. It wasn't the man he supported, even though he liked Zander, but it was the actual charity he was currently there for. He felt strongly about the cause. Every penny raised went to help child victims of sex trafficking to start new lives. It was an issue that was close to his heart for many reasons. This particular event was a bit different from the rest. Louder, for sure. Rowdier. Saul Gabris, Zander's righthand Atlantic City man, had definitely put a twist on the usual boring speeches. Cutler had to admit, a four-night pirate cruise was a fun idea for people who knew how to party. No one knew how to consume copious amounts of alcohol while writing blank checks the way the elite did. It was interesting to watch the upper crust lose their inhibitions.

Cutler had always been a people watcher. He found Saul's man especially interesting. The guy smiled so much, it was easy to believe he didn't have a single thought in his head. Yet he had snagged Saul Gabris. That was a feat. Saul was a suspicious, mean, and bitter bastard. The way his gaze stayed locked on the man who'd won him was almost frightening. It made Cutler wonder if the poor guy was safe. He looked like the type to get eaten alive.

While trying not to look obvious, Cutler worked his way through the crowd until he ended up next to him at the bar. He glanced over and pretended surprise. "Oh, you're with Saul, right?"

Sexy gray eyes turned his way. The smile never dimmed. "Yeah." He held out his hand. "I'm Case."

Cutler shook. "Cutler Maine."

"Nice to meet you."

Cutler dipped his chin. "Where did you lose Saul to?"

Case pointed toward a group of men across the room. Saul looked deep in conversation. "He's there."

Cutler decided to test the waters. Not that Case's safety was any of his business, nor did he have a plan if it turned out Case was in trouble. "He's a lucky man. Saul has a notorious temper, yet you look... happy." Cutler hadn't truly known where he was going with that. He didn't know how to vocalize his concerns without incurring Saul's wrath. Plus, what did he really think he would do?

Case looked confused. "People think Saul has a temper?"

Cutler made a dismissive gesture. "It's just a rumor."

Case's expression cleared. "Oh. Well, there's a lot of those, I suppose. When we first met, I was warned to stay away from him because he makes people disappear." Case motioned toward himself. "Theory disproved," he said with a laugh.

Cutler pasted on his fakest smile. "It seems so." Before Cutler could say anything else, a too drunk guy snagged Case's attention. The man immediately turned handsy. Case looked more than capable of handling himself, but Cutler's gaze sought Saul in the crowd again. He wondered if he should step in. The murderous rage written on Saul's face had Cutler sipping his drink and taking a step back. A fight would definitely liven up this party.

"What's that smile about?"

Cutler turned his head at the question, finding a familiar man with a sexy body waiting for his attention. "Anticipating some action," Cutler answered honestly. He loved drama as much as the next person, as long as it was someone else's.

Green eyes swept down Cutler's body. "Same."

Cutler didn't think they had the same action in mind. Still, Special Agent Gable Johnson had Cutler's attention. This party would get wilder one way or another. A naughty CIA agent with a penchant for turning up in his life unexpectedly sounded like just the trick he needed.

Oddly, these reconnaissance jobs were Gable's favorite. He had always been good at blending in, going unnoticed. He was a bit of a chameleon like that. As a liaison between the CIA and FBI, he did a lot of various things. Sometimes, he might buy drugs from biker gangs. Other days, he rubbed elbows with society's most elite. That was the case now. Everyone on the list of Atlantic City's most wanted was in attendance—from the most sought after and richest bachelors to the CIA's top ten list of most wanted criminals. Those two lists were a Venn diagram, which was also a solid circle.

One thing he had learned about the uber wealthy was they were strange. They loved to party, but they were also bored with everything. That combination led to events like this one: a four-night pirate cruise to raise money for a children's charity. It was a good cause. The charity saved countless children from sex trafficking. None of these people cared about that. They just wanted to dress like pirates, get shitfaced, fuck, and then they would write a big check. Everyone went home happy... and hungover.

Gable had watched the drama all night while sticking to the sidelines. Then a familiar face had cut through the crowd. Gable's entire body had gone on alert. Cutler Maine likely had at least ten years on Gable. The last time Gable had seen him had been inside the CIA's Alabama headquarters, for reasons Gable still didn't quite understand. A leather jacket had hidden his sexy body. The guy had light blue eyes and a wicked smile that had completely distracted Gable from the reason for Cutler's visit. Now here he was again... the sexiest older gentleman Gable had ever seen. Gable honestly didn't know his age. He was likely close to fifty. With one look at him, Gable's thirty-five didn't feel that distant.

While Gable had watched, Cutler leaned against the bar, speaking with a much younger man who was too beautiful for his own good. Gable thought his name was Case. While Gable wasn't totally positive of his name, he was a thousand percent aware the guy was dating the host of the event, Saul Gabris. That was a deadly endeavor for Cutler. Saul had been on the CIA's radar for years, but the guy was untouchable. His connections had connections. Plus, Saul never made anyone innocent disappear. It was hard to care about the type of people who saw Saul as their last sight on earth. There were just some things Gable had no trouble turning a blind eye to. Saul was one of those things.

As Gable had looked on, Saul's icy stare latched onto the spot where his man received too much attention. As Saul had headed Cutler's way, Gable had moved too, in case he needed to protect a CIA asset. Cutler had his own set of connections that kept him out of prison, but he also—occasionally—worked with the CIA on freelance. Gable couldn't let him get hurt. He had made it to Cutler just in time to see Saul unleash his fury on a different guest. The overly inebriated man had gotten handsy. Gable was oddly grateful for the douche. He had unwittingly saved Cutler from Saul's wrath.

Now, Gable had the attention of the one man at this party he should avoid like the plague. Unlike everyone else, Cutler knew Gable worked for the CIA. While a vast majority of people there wouldn't care, Gable still had a job to do. For a moment, he let Cutler's sexy eyes and wicked mouth distract him. Unfortunately, his prey chose that moment to appear. Gable's gaze slid past Cutler. "Please excuse me. As much as I'd like to play, duty calls."

"That's too bad. You're eerily good at slipping from my clutches."

Gable bit back a laugh as he fell into character. He had a long night ahead of him.

Cutler watched Gable transform before his eyes. He rolled up the sleeves of his white pirate shirt, exposing his tattoo-covered forearms. Gable went from bland wallflower to sexy soul wrecker in an instant. After undoing the top two buttons on his shirt, letting everyone see the heavily tattooed chest underneath, his expression changed. No longer was he the straight-laced CIA agent Cutler had met by chance months earlier. He was out to break hearts... or someone's bed. Pity it wasn't his.

With another devilish look his way, Cutler watched Gable dive into the crowd. He bumped into a guy who looked vaguely familiar, but Cutler couldn't place him. Anyone else watching might've thought the collision had been accidental. Cutler knew better. He watched the man's eyes turn hungry. Gable's gaze swept the man's body with interest. The pair shifted closer. Cutler's phone buzzed.

With a sigh, he dug his phone from his pocket. He very much feared it was time for him to get to work too. As an elimination specialist, he didn't always know his target until he was in place. He was in place.

X: *Job canceled. Plans have changed. An agent is onsite to takeover.*

That was a bit irritating. He was two days into this four-night bullshit. If the CIA continued wasting his time, he had higher bidders. His phone buzzed again before he had time for his mood to darken further.

X: *Pay will be unaffected. Confirmation of receipt is needed.*

Cutler's shoulders relaxed. He was cool with getting paid for a cruise with zero expectations. Now he could relax and enjoy himself without fear he would have to kill the person he fucked. It was a win in his books.

Cutler: *New orders confirmed.*

His gaze moved back to where Gable charmed his new friend. It seemed this was his target. Truth be told, he was a little disappointed it wasn't the handsy guy who had accosted Case. Still, Cutler found a barstool and sat. Now that he knew who had earned the wrath of the U.S. government, Cutler wasn't sure he should leave Gable unprotected. While Gable's cut body screamed he could take care of himself, Gable was the white knight type. Cutler had no such bullshit holding him in check. He had seen the underbelly of the world and no longer cared if it burned. There was nothing he wouldn't do. His conscience had been stripped from him a long time ago. Now he lived by his rules for the highest bidder. He would keep Gable safe.

CHAPTER TWO

THE POUNDING IN GABLE'S head spoke volumes about how far he had gone to pry information from Warren Legion. Warren was the right hand of the devil. That much the CIA knew. For years, they had tried to figure out who pulled his strings, with no luck. Whoever financed his deeds had connections and was damn good at being invisible. Warren was their only ticket to his boss. Gable had been forced to drink the man under the table to avoid going to bed with him. It wasn't that Warren was a bad-looking guy. Gable never wanted to go that far for his country. He had managed to slip a small listening device into Warren's wallet after helping him to bed. The dude had immediately passed out. The high-tech device was small enough that he doubted Warren would notice it for a while. Now Gable had to vanish before crossing paths with him again.

Under the cover of darkness, Gable donned his diving suit. Transport waited a mile out. It was times like these that being a retired Navy SEAL came in handy. It would take him less than half an hour to swim to meet the waiting boat. He would be in bed before morning.

"I take it you got what you came for?"

Gable froze as the words cut through the dark. He turned. Cutler appeared from the shadows. His shoulders relaxed. "I don't know what answer you're looking for, but it's a hundred times better for a guest who was never on the list to disappear than a prominent one. Fewer police and disruption of a worthy cause."

"Less wrath from the wrong people."

Gable smiled. "Exactly."

Cutler's gaze swept down Gable's body. "You intend to swim back?"

"Are you worried about me?"

The heat in Cutler's gaze didn't lessen. "More curious than anything."

Gable wasn't sure having Cutler's curiosity was a good thing. A door opened nearby. Before Gable had time to decide what to do, Cutler hauled him into a darkened corner. His body hid Gable's. Their faces were inches apart. Footsteps moved closer, so did Cutler. When it became obvious they would be spotted, Cutler had his back.

"Public displays of affection make people uncomfortable." That was all the warning Gable got before Cutler's mouth covered his. Then he forgot why they were there. Objectively, it was a skillful kiss. Cutler could definitely do things with his tongue. The sound of a door snapping closed had Cutler stepping back. For a moment, they simply stared at each other.

Gable broke first. "I need to go before I lose my window."

Cutler moved from his path. "I know you can find my number with one text. Let me know when you've made it wherever you're going. Just so I don't worry," he added, sounding dry and unaffected by their kiss.

With a dip of his chin, Gable made his way to the railing and climbed over. Without looking back, he eased himself down a set of wire ropes before diving into the cold water.

His training took over, clearing his mind. He had a goal. Gable couldn't look back.

Cutler stood on the deck for much longer than necessary. Twenty minutes passed while he stared at the water, wondering if Gable survived the dive. He couldn't imagine the courage it would take to leap from the ship in the middle of the night into nothing. Fuck. The guy was hot. His phone buzzed, distracting him. He checked the face. It was a text from an unknown number.

Unknown: *This is Gable. I made it.*

Cutler's eyebrows rose. He quickly saved Gable as a contact before responding.

Cutler: *Damn. That was fast. SEAL?*

Gable: *In an another life, yes.*

Cutler: *I'm glad you're safe.*

After putting his phone away, Cutler headed for his room. That kiss weighed on him. He would be lying if he said he hadn't purposely taken advantage of the situation, but he hadn't been prepared for that fucking kiss.

A few months back, Cutler had jumped on his Harley and headed south. During his trip, his boss had set up a meeting with someone he thought Cutler should meet. It seemed the CIA needed men like him for contracted, legal and U.S. sanctioned exterminations. After Zander had assured his safety from arrest, Cutler had agreed to a meeting at the Mobile, Alabama CIA headquarters. Ten minutes in, Gable had burst in with an urgent message for his contact.

Cutler had noticed his tattooed hands first. They had looked rugged and sexy and completely at odds with his business suit. Then Gable had looked Cutler's way. Cutler had been immediately reminded of those super-hero movies where the character's only disguise was glasses. Gable had actually been wearing glasses that day. His green eyes had sparkled with intelligence. Cutler had been struck with a desire to unwrap Gable like a present to discover what he hid. They'd exchanged introductions and a very brief flirtation before Gable had been called away as quickly as he came. That was the extent of them before tonight. Cutler hadn't expected to see the guy again. Now his interest was fully piqued. His phone buzzed again as he opened the door to his cabin.

Gable: *Now you know my story. What's yours?*

A smile exploded across Cutler's face.

Cutler: *I absolutely do not know your story, but I'll make you a deal. If we run into each other again, I'll tell you mine if you tell me yours.*

Gable: *Deal.*

Cutler didn't stop smiling while he undressed. While he doubted they would see each other again, since they lived over a thousand miles apart, he enjoyed the idea. That kiss would keep him warm tonight. Then, who knew? Stranger things had happened.

CHAPTER THREE

THE SCENT OF COFFEE permeated the air. Cutler savored the smell as he enjoyed his scone. He did everything alone. Always had. At fifty, he had long given up the dream of trusting anyone enough to let them close enough to love him. He had made the mistake of loving someone once. He still had nightmares about it. Sitting inside a packed cafe, surrounded by chatting people, these were the moments when he felt the lack of company the most. Not always. Just sometimes, he would look around and realize he was the only person who sat alone. That was why he tried to keep his gaze locked on his phone, reading the news or doing puzzles. There was nothing for him in the world surrounding him. Some people were just like that. Destined to be alone.

A shadow fell over the table a moment before the chair across from him filled. Cutler looked up to find Gable's smiling face. Cutler's eyebrows rose. "This is becoming too common to be a coincidence."

Gable's smile grew. "I assure you it is."

Cutler found that hard to believe, but he would entertain this. He set his phone aside. "Considering we live more than a thousand miles apart, I call bullshit."

"Actually, I live here now. I had a slight career change shortly after we met."

He had Cutler's attention. Cutler leaned back in his chair and eyed Gable. "You've left the CIA?"

Gable shook his head. "I didn't actually work for the CIA when we met. Officially, I worked for the FBI back then. I was just a liaison between the two agencies, so I split my days between the headquarters. Then, making a long story short, I got a new boss at the FBI. An order I received before he took the position put me in the path of his wrath. I thought it best to remove myself from the situation and take a job I'd been offered with the CIA here in Atlantic City. So, this is where I've been for a few months now."

Cutler inspected him. He was dressed casually today. A t-shirt showed off his muscular arms and intricate tattoos. He truly was a sexy guy despite his almost military haircut.

Cutler wasn't a fan of anything the least bit authoritarian. "You look relaxed today."

"I have the day off. When I ordered my coffee, I couldn't believe my eyes when I saw you sitting here. You know what this means, right?"

Cutler lifted his eyebrows in question.

An evil-looking smile stretched Gable's lips. "You have to tell me your story. A deal is a deal."

Damn. He had said that. "I can't imagine this is the place." His admissions couldn't be made in public.

Gable eyed him, as if trying to decide if Cutler only tried to back out of their deal or if he was serious. "Let's take this to go, then. My place isn't that far. I could make you lunch."

A laugh escaped him. "I don't know. By your own admission, I don't know you. Should I go home with a stranger?"

Gable's eyes danced with laughter. "I feel certain you can handle yourself."

Cutler grabbed his coffee and the helmet that sat on the chair next to him. "Lead the way."

Gable's gaze dropped to the helmet. "Is the Harley out front yours?"

Cutler nodded. "My midlife crisis mobile," he admitted with a laugh. A little because he needed to highlight the age difference between them. That kiss haunted him, but he doubted it was the same for someone so much younger than him.

"Good choice." Gable never stopped smiling. "Maybe we could go for a ride sometime."

He sounded genuine. Cutler didn't know what to think. "Sounds great. Anytime you want. Except today," he added with a laugh. "I don't have a second helmet with me."

"Actually, I meant I have a bike too."

Great. Cutler was back to being confused. He didn't understand if Gable tried striking up a friendship or something more. "Awesome. I can't wait to take a look."

With a huge grin, Gable fell into a spiel about specs and customization. Cutler nodded along as they made the walk to the parking lot. Cutler put on his helmet. Gable motioned toward a nearby SUV that looked exactly like it belonged to the CIA.

"Just follow me. I'm seriously like five minutes from here."

"Sounds good." Cutler straddled his bike and crossed his fingers this wasn't a mistake. He was too old to make a fool of himself. Gable had him dangerously close to wanting to do just that.

The thing about spending years as an agent was, it made him entirely too good at lying. Gable had known exactly where to find Cutler. He had since the moment Cutler returned from the cruise two weeks ago. Gable had just been trying to decide the best way to arrange an organic-looking meeting. Plus, he wasn't totally sure what he wanted from this. He found Cutler incredibly hot. Gable had a feeling the guy was intelligent and interesting. He just wanted to see more. Plus, that goddamn kiss. Wow.

Still, he used the five-minute drive to berate himself for immediately inviting the man back to his place. He honestly wanted to know why Cutler had been inside the CIA headquarters and in Alabama, of all places. But he totally understood not being able to talk about work in public. Next to no one knew anything about him, and it would always be that way. That hard truth made it impossible to have a genuine relationship. He wanted someone he could be real with.

As Gable turned into his driveway, the garage door slid open. He pulled into one bay before jumping out and hitting the button on the second so Cutler could park next to his bike. The doors slowly closed as Cutler climbed from his motorcycle and pulled off his helmet. He walked a circle around Gable's Harley.

"Damn. That's badass."

Gable's chest expanded with pride and spilled into his smile. "Thanks. It's my midlife crisis mobile."

Cutler barked out a loud laugh that made the ridiculous statement worthwhile. "Surely you have awhile for that yet."

Gable shrugged. "Between the tattoos and the bike, my mom keeps asking what I'll have left to do when I start worrying about growing old. I tell her I'm already old and then she punches me in the arm."

Cutler's smile never dimmed. "Good for her. Tell her to hit you from me too next time. If you think you're old, I can't imagine what you think of me."

"I don't even know how old you are."

Cutler's eyes flashed with humor and intelligence. "Liar. I guarantee you know everything about me you could possibly dig up. Otherwise, you never would've invited me to your home."

"True." Gable motioned for Cutler to follow him inside. He spoke over his shoulder as he went. "With that said, there's not much to be found about you. It's almost like you didn't even exist before twenty years ago."

"That's because I didn't."

Gable toed off his shoes inside the back door. Cutler followed his lead and pulled off his boots. Gable led him to the kitchen table. He didn't continue until they were seated, and he could watch every nuance of Cutler's expression. Gable was good at his job. He could read anyone. "If you didn't exist, then who are you?"

A way too sexy smile touched Cutler's lips. He looked deadly in that moment in a way Gable never expected. While he knew exactly what Cutler did for a living, this was the first time he recognized he stared at a killer. When he spoke, an entirely different accent emerged. "Cheslav Makarov." His voice automatically returned to perfect flat

American. "But I haven't been that person in a long time."

Gable's mind stuttered for a moment. "Why do I know that name?"

Cutler stood. "That's probably my cue."

The memory struck. "Holy shit. You're the son of Antinko Momarov."

Cutler looked uncomfortable and ready to bolt.

Gable motioned toward the seat Cutler had vacated. "Sit. It's fine. I'm surprised, of course, but if you're here and you were allowed to walk in and freely walk out of CIA headquarters, I assume you're nothing like him."

Despite still looking unsure, Cutler sat. "It's okay if you don't want me here. I'm very accustomed to being the only son of Russia's most feared mafia leader. I've seen and done a lot of terrible things, but I'm not him, nor could I stop him."

Gable was fascinated. "But you did, right? Didn't you testify against him?"

Cutler gave a jerky nod. It was obvious he expected Gable to reject him at any moment. "He hurt children, and I could never. The things he did and helped others do were unspeakable. So, I did what I had to do and then I was smuggled to America by a connection in California."

"Zander Kapra." Gable couldn't keep the know-it-all out of his voice. Everyone knew who ran the west coast, and they were lucky it was a good man. Zander also had a hard-on for destroying all things child sex crime related. The guy would help Cutler. In fact, he could protect him in ways no government ever could. No one had even known what Antinko's son looked like. Antinko had kept his only child secreted away from the public eye. Gable had also been a child back in the day of Cutler taking him down, so there was zero chance he would have recognized him. He had so many questions, he didn't know where to start.

"Why were you at CIA headquarters the day we met?"

Cutler shrugged. "I was taking a road trip when Zander asked me to meet with a friend of his at the agency. You know what I do. He wanted me to do it for him."

It was funny the way they skirted around the fact that he killed people. "You must've lived an interesting life."

A laugh burst from Cutler. "Damn. Just call me old next time."

Gable had to concede that comment had sounded like something he would say to a grandparent. "I didn't mean it like that. Your life has just been very diverse. I can't imagine all the things you've seen."

Cutler's smile fell. "You don't want to imagine the things I've seen." His expression immediately shifted again, as if becoming someone new. "But what about you? That swim time a couple of weeks ago was impressive as hell."

A swell of pride rose inside Gable. It was out of his control. He didn't get praised often. "Top of my class," Gable admitted with a chuckle. He looked around. "So, I'd planned a disgustingly cheesy homemade mac-n-cheese for lunch, but I can make sandwiches if you'd prefer."

"I like cheese."

"Good." Gable wasn't ready for Cutler to leave. He was fascinated. He needed to know more.

CHAPTER FOUR

THE LUNCH HE HAD spent with Gable didn't ease Cutler's confusion, not even a hair. They had spent the entire day together. Lunch had turned into talking all day before going for a ride. They had sat on the beach for a while and talked for hours before going to dinner at a small Mexican restaurant off the beaten path. It had been one of the best nights Cutler could recall having in years. Then it had ended in a strange sort of handshake, half hug thing that had felt awkward as hell. In fact, even through revealing his past, that goodbye had still been the most uncomfortable moment of the entire experience. It didn't feel like a date. That was disappointing.

Cutler kept his eye focused on the scope of his high-powered rifle, waiting for the perfect shot. His mind wasn't where it should be. A shipping container filled with victims waiting to be sold sat on the docks. Two armed guards stood nearby, waiting for the next leg of transport. Cutler needed all players in place. It did no good to take out the guards before the next ones arrived. That would only spook the next round of garbage, possibly bringing reinforcements before the victim recovery team could begin gathering the kids for medical treatment. These, in between moments where he did nothing but wait, always took every ounce of his patience. He wasn't unaffected. This wasn't just some cold, emotionless job Cutler did. Cutler wanted these guys dead.

He had been the only child of a monster. While Antinko Momarov had access to countless children at his fingertips, and savored them every chance he got, Cutler had been his favorite toy. Maybe he had also drowned his son in everything money could buy, but that bullshit meant nothing when living in a constant nightmare. Cutler wasn't his son any longer. He was Cutler Maine. Cutler killed people like him now. His head needed to be here, where he could make a difference. Why hadn't he at least tried kissing Gable last night? Gable hadn't balked on the ship. He might not have last night either. Why was he acting like a nervous teenager with a crush? Was it the age difference? He was never insecure like this. Cutler was being ridiculous. He needed to work.

The back doors swung wide on the shipping container as headlights neared the dock. Through his scope, Cutler saw the huddled dirty children, shaking and wide eyed. He hated they were about to witness one more horror. Hopefully, it would be for the last time for them. Two large box trucks arrived. Men poured from the front of each. Even from his distant hiding spot, Cutler heard the loud laughter. The men were hyped to try the goods before taking them any farther. It wouldn't be happening.

Cutler took a breath and lightly squeezed the trigger. One by one, he moved with lightning speed, taking out each target before they could run. He started with the visibly armed men, but no one else had time to even wonder what happened before it was their turn. As quickly as they fell, the recovery and cleanup teams swooped in, shielding the kids from the gruesome sight.

Cutler didn't watch. He broke down his weapon and repacked his gear before making his way to his truck. It was just another night. Once he climbed behind the wheel, he pulled out his phone.

Cutler: *Job complete.*

J: *Awaiting the mandatory two confirmations.*

While waiting, Cutler stared at nothing and went over the day again. He'd had at least four chances to make a move. Several times, they had been close, and the conversation had trailed off while they stared at each other. Surely Gable felt that too.

J: *Confirmation complete. Wire transfer in progress.*

Cutler pulled up his offshore bank account on his phone and checked. A new deposit with a lot of zeros appeared. He would do this for free, but money was money.

There was no guarantee his father's people wouldn't find him someday. He would need the assets to run.

Cutler: *Received.*

Another night. Another successful operation. He didn't feel any better. Cutler kept staring at nothing. He needed to leave. Soon the place would be buzzing with people, ensuring the scene disappeared like it had never happened. He liked his anonymity. Fuck it.

Cutler: *Have dinner with me tomorrow night. A date, in case I'm not being clear.*

He sent the text before letting himself think. Then he covered his eyes from the horror of his words. He sounded cold and ridiculous. Cutler was just so damn unsure over everything. If Gable said no, then fine. He would know, and they would never see each other again. Cutler couldn't keep dealing with this confusion.

Gable: *Was today not a date?*

A smile exploded across Cutler's face.

Cutler: *I wasn't sure since it didn't end with the kiss I would've liked.*

There. It was easier to be honest via text.

Gable: *That was my fault. I wasn't sure that's what you wanted since things felt awkward as we said goodbye. I'd love to have dinner together tomorrow.*

At least Cutler knew he hadn't imagined things. Their parting had been uncomfortable.

Cutler: *Good. I'll pick you up at seven. Will that work?*

Gable: *That's perfect since I get off at six.*

He had known that. That was the only reason he suggested such a late meal. Cutler knew everything about Gable. He never spent time with anyone he didn't fully research. Since finding out Gable had relocated to Atlantic City, Cutler had made a call and had a file on him in under half an hour. He knew everything.

Cutler: *I'll see you then.*

Giddiness ran through Cutler as he started his truck. A smile pulled at his lips. They were going on a real date. He could go home now and sleep. His mind needed the rest.

Gable paced the floor and went over the entire day in his head. Why was he such a coward when it came to Cutler? Gable worked undercover, taking down drug dealers and murderers, for fuck's sake. This one guy had him fucked up. Several times throughout the day, he had thought they were about to kiss before Gable caught himself finding a new topic to turn the tide. He was dumb as hell, sabotaging himself. Jesus. He really liked Cutler. The guy was sexy and smart. He was a bit dark and mysterious. Good God. He gave Gable butterflies. Gable felt younger than he had in years. He also felt stupid for his inability to be the smooth adult he normally was. Gable just needed to chill.

He stopped in the middle of his living room and stared at nothing. All he saw was Cutler's laughing eyes. Goddamn. It had been a long time since he had been this attracted to anyone. They had a date tomorrow night. He could get that kiss this time. Gable would because he couldn't be a pussy for two days in a row. Even Cutler had pointed out how that kiss hadn't happened. Goddamn it.

Gable sat, feeling defeated. He relaxed into the couch and closed his eyes. God, it had been years since he felt this way. In his line of work, too often he played a role. Everything felt fake all the time. Today, everything had been real. Every smile and laugh had been Gable. Not whoever he was expected to be. It wasn't like drinking Warren under the table, attempting to avoid unwanted sex. Cutler had his attention. He couldn't forget that kiss. If Cutler could split his attention between kissing Gable and ensure Gable didn't get caught leaving the ship, Gable couldn't imagine how amazing that mouth must be when Cutler gave someone his full attention. Gable went hard just thinking about it.

Damn. He missed being touched. It had been way too long. He spent more time than he liked trying to avoid sex with people he didn't want. He wanted Cutler. Gable popped the button on his jeans, trying to adjust the growing discomfort of his dick trying to climb out of his pants. He had so many questions. What did Cutler like? Was he a top or bottom? Gable's hand slid inside his underwear. He was good with whatever. Years ago, he had strictly been a top. Then an undercover mission had put him in the position of having to fake being a virgin and a bottom. Since he wasn't really faking the part about never bottoming for anyone, he was grateful the target had a kink for being the man who showed men how much pleasure their bodies could endure. A new side of him had been unleashed. Now Gable would take whatever role his partner needed. He could see himself straddling Cutler's lap.

Gable squeezed his cock and then stroked. He bet Cutler was fucking amazing on his knees. The way that tongue had moved inside his mouth. Goddamn. Gable stroked faster, picturing Cutler staring up at him as he bobbed on Gable's dick. Soon his thoughts turned too desperate and depraved for Gable to focus. He strained against his palm. His ragged breathing filled the otherwise quiet room. He tugged faster, needing relief from this madness.

A cry tore from Gable's lips. Cum coated his shirt as he savored the orgasm that owned him. Cutler's name fell from his lips without his permission. His body went limp as he tried catching his breath. Gable looked down at the mess he had made. Tomorrow. He would get that fucking kiss tomorrow. Then they would make this a reality. He couldn't settle for less.

CHAPTER FIVE

THE DOORBELL RANG, AND Gable swiped his sweating palms on his jeans. He had lived in fear all day of being stood up. There was no reason for Cutler to keep their date. There was also no reason for Gable to think he wouldn't show. He was just nervous. Cutler seemed great. Dating wasn't his biggest strength. He wanted things to go well.

As Gable opened the door, the delicious scent of Cutler's cologne hit first. He fought the urge to smile like an idiot. Cutler looked sexy as sin. "Hey."

Cutler stepped inside. "Hey." That was it. Cutler overcame him before the word died on his lips. Their mouths met. All good sense fled. Then Gable made a fatal mistake. His hands collided with Cutler's torso. He got his first feel of the incredible body Cutler kept hidden beneath his clothes. His soul wept for more. He had to have more.

"I swear I'll take you to dinner." There was no fake American accent. It was as if Gable had him too turned on to focus.

"I don't give a shit."

Cutler held the back of Gable's head, controlling their kiss. Gable found his way beneath Cutler's shirt. He had to touch bare skin. A stuttered breath escaped him when he felt the softness over hard muscle. They couldn't go to dinner. Gable leaked pre-cum inside his underwear.

"I didn't plan things this way."

Gable needed him to stop talking and fuck him. "I don't care."

It seemed the second reassurance was all Cutler needed. His hands found the button on Gable's jeans. He popped it open and slid down his zipper. A sexy growl escaped him as his hand dove inside Gable's under-wear. Gable moaned as he squeezed. All good sense fled. Gable tore at Cutler's jeans. He wanted to touch Cutler too. They kissed while tugging and pulled at each other's clothes as they moved toward the couch. There was no way they would make it to the bedroom.

Everything looked hazy as Cutler ripped open his wallet and pulled half the shit out while finding a condom. No oxygen reached Gable's brain. He half-ass noticed Cutler tearing into a small packet of lube. Gable was past the point of caring. He was desperate. Gable felt almost frantic with lust. Then Cutler thrust, impaling him. They froze.

Gable was on his back with no memory of how he ended up there. Cutler had one arm bracing himself on the arm of the couch. He stared down at Gable and thrust again. The steady way he held Gable's gaze fucked with Gable's head. He couldn't look away. It was as if Cutler needed Gable to recognize who fucked him. There was no chance he could see anyone else. Cutler was in his head. Everything felt extreme and powerful. The moment seemed pivotal, as if Gable's life had just changed in a way he didn't understand yet. He felt the shift in his chest.

Cutler slowly lowered his head. Their lips met. This time, Gable's breath shook. He recognized he had just been owned. Claimed. This wasn't just sex. Cutler rocked inside him at the perfect angle to steal every thought. Gable dug his heel into the couch as leverage as he fought to get closer. Everything vanished except his need to come. Their kiss turned violent again as Cutler's thrusts quickened. They were so focused, the only sound was their bodies slapping and ragged breaths. All the sensations grew to a crescendo. Gable's muscles tensed so hard, he could snap a tendon. He held his breath and focused everything on the building tension. Then, bliss. Cries filled the air. Gable didn't even recognize the sounds that came from him. Cutler buried his face against Gable's chest and thrust hard, riding Gable's orgasm. Desperate sounds vibrated against Gable's skin. Pride filled him as Cutler blew. Every second and sound seared into memory, cementing itself as the sexiest encounter in Gable's life. He had never made anyone lose control like that. It was empowering. His ego had never been as big.

He didn't know which of them laughed first, but once one started, they both shook with laughter. Cutler kissed his cheek between chuckles. "Oh, God. I swear I didn't plan this. I don't know what happened."

Gable couldn't stop smiling. "We should probably order in for dinner."

Cutler shook harder with laughter. His chin lifted. Gable's heart sighed at the happiness in Cutler's gorgeous eyes. This wasn't a one-time thing. He wanted this. He wanted Cutler.

After grabbing a blanket and pillows from Gable's bedroom, they made a pallet on the floor. They ordered food and lounged while spending the night talking. Cutler felt comfortable for the first time in his life. It wasn't the peace he experienced by the silence of his life since leaving Russia. This was new. It was a shared calm. Until that moment, he hadn't realized that was exactly what he sought. His life had been too hard and loud. Violent. This was different. He couldn't put his finger on it quite yet but Cutler didn't want whatever this was to stop.

"I see most of your things are still in boxes. Are you hoping not to stay?"

A sexy chuckle fell from Gable's lips at Cutler's question. "It's not that. I'm just lazy. This place is smaller than where I lived back home. Obviously, it's a hell of a lot more expensive to live here than Alabama. I have so much shit with nowhere to put it. Until I started packing and thinking about moving everything over a thousand miles away, I didn't realize how much crap I own." Gable laughed. "A million times I wondered why I owned half the things I do, but I still just packed it anyway. The task feels daunting."

On his side, with his head propped up on his hand, Cutler stared at Gable. He truly looked defeated at the idea of unpacking. "I have the opposite problem at my place. When I left Russia, I left with the clothes on my back. Then, when I finally made it to the states, I drifted from safe house to safe house for years until I fully became Cutler Maine. I suppose I haven't owned much for so long, I just don't buy anything anymore. My house is practically empty."

"Oh, good. I know where I can store my stuff." Gable's eyes swam with laughter as he made the claim.

Cutler shrugged. "Feel free. I have the room."

Gable scooted closer. He moved aside the basket of fries that sat between them so he could get even closer. His fingertips skimmed Cutler's side, making goosebumps skirt Cutler's skin, but his gaze never wavered from holding Cutler's stare. "I was joking, but I love that you talk like this wasn't a one-night stand for you."

Cutler's eyebrows shot up. That thought hadn't even crossed his mind, but it had obviously crossed Gable's. "Was that even a concern?"

Gable shrugged. He kissed the corner of Cutler's mouth, as if trying to distract him. "I never want to assume anything." He swiped another sweet kiss across Cutler's lips. "I work an unappealing job. People don't like that I can't share what I'm doing. No one wants to be with someone who has to keep secrets."

Cutler rolled. He straddled Gable's body as he toppled Gable onto his back. With his hands braced on either side of Gable's head, he stole the kiss he wanted. He didn't like being teased. Once satisfied, he pulled away enough to hold Gable's stare. "My entire existence is a secret. I have a whole past I can't share. I'll never ask for more of you than you can give. But I want what I can have of you. This was by no means a one-night stand. I'm not built that way. I want this."

The way Gable stared up at him—like he was filled with the same hope for the future Cutler felt—warmed Cutler's chest. "I want this too. Your past doesn't matter to me. I want your future."

Goddamn. That was the hottest thing anyone had ever said to him. Cutler lowered his head and tasted Gable's lips again. Their kiss felt like a promise. They were starting something. Cutler felt it in his soul. He couldn't wait to see what happened next.

Chapter Six

Smoke wafted in Gable's face. He hated the smell of cigars. The sounds of slot machines assailed him. The flashing lights and noise had never been his thing. Gable lifted the corner of his cards and checked his numbers. He tapped the table, asking for one more.

"Mr. Gabris would like to see you." The gigantic guard spoke close to his ear, making it clear it wasn't a request.

That was exactly what Gable had been waiting to hear. He stood. "Keep my chips as a tip."

The dealer nodded, and Gable followed his escort. This was what he had been working toward for the past hour. He couldn't go to Saul like they were friends. No one could know they knew each other. It was important he keep his identity under the radar. Saul ran three casinos in Atlantic City. The richest and most depraved visited these places. It would likely be a common occurrence for him to play his part here.

Inside Saul's back office, eerie light eyes waited. While seated behind his desk, Saul watched him enter the room. He didn't speak until the door closed, leaving them alone.

"Gable. What do I owe today's visit to my establishment?"

Gable sat without being invited. "I wanted to thank you for allowing me access to the cruise. Also, congratulations. I heard you asked Case to marry you and he accepted."

A hint of a smile touched Saul's lips. The man was dangerous and scary. He had made more people vanish than the Bermuda Triangle. That small smile proved his soft spot for his future husband. It was good to see the guy was human. "Thank you. We're looking forward to a bright future. As for the cruise, were you successful?"

Gable dipped his chin. He couldn't answer further.

"I hear you've been reassigned to my town. Does that mean I can anticipate your presence on the casino floor more often?"

"Likely." Gable braced himself for any reaction. Saul didn't have to tolerate him. The law might look the other way, allowing Saul to run his businesses as he pleased. That didn't mean any alphabet organization had any jurisdiction here. They weren't safe if Saul said they weren't.

Saul eyed him.

Gable held his stare, despite how uncomfortable it was.

Finally, Saul blew out an irritated-sounding sigh. "I expect anything you do will not interrupt any operations here. You will not implicate us as helping you in any way. Our customers should be allowed to spend their money freely here without your interference. Anything you discover here can wait until you hit the parking lot for arrests. Think of my casinos as neutral grounds. I won't interfere with you if you don't interfere with me." His gaze somehow got more intense. "This is nonnegotiable."

Gable nodded. "I have no objections. It's imperative no one knows what I do, so I don't make arrests. I'm just an infiltrator."

Saul leaned back in his chair and steepled his fingers. His mouth lifted in one corner. "Is that what you're doing with Cutler?"

He reacted before his brain churned out a thought. A smile exploded across his face at the sound of Cutler's name. It was too late to lie, nor did he want to. Plus, it was obvious Saul already knew everything. "No. That's personal."

A scary-sounding chuckle rumbled from Saul. "And real from the looks of it."

Gable didn't respond, but he also didn't stop smiling. "Are we cool?"

Saul didn't answer. He spent a moment looking thoughtful. His mouth opened before he snapped it shut again. It was obvious he fought himself. Finally, he leaned forward again. "You know Cutler isn't who he seems, right?"

Honestly, Gable was a little moved by Saul's warning. It seemed Saul was a sucker for love. That was good to know. He knew Saul's weakness. "I know about his past."

With a sharp nod, Saul stood. "Good. Cutler has more than earned the right to be free from pain and be happy."

That statement punched Gable in the chest. Maybe he didn't know quite as much as Saul did. A terrible realization overcame Gable. Cutler had been raised by a monster. He had only spoken of what he witnessed. Not what he had endured. Gable seriously doubted—son or not—he had been spared from the clutches of a predator. The thought made Gable's chest hurt. Since Saul waited for a response, Gable managed a fake smile. "Agreed."

Saul moved toward the door. "Then I think we're through here. Enjoy your day." A wicked-looking smile touched his lips. "Feel free to lose your money here anytime."

Gable snorted, but he realized he liked Saul. Despite everything, he was genuine. There wasn't enough of that in the world, especially in Gable's business.

Cutler lit a candle on the table just in time for the doorbell. He smirked. It was out of his control. His pride and ego swelled every time he thought of Gable. His doubts didn't stand a chance against the memory of Gable beneath him. The desperation Cutler had felt for him had been equally matched. There was no faking their frantic pursuit of sexual gratification. Gable wanted him as much as Cutler craved Gable. There was something between them.

He didn't want to keep Gable waiting. Cutler rushed to the door. Once there, he took a breath so it wouldn't look like he had sprinted to answer. When he opened the door, there was no hiding his happiness. Gable stood on the other side holding a bouquet of multicolored flowers.

He held them out to Cutler. "Surprise."

God. He was perfect. Cutler accepted his gift. "Thank you. These are gorgeous."

Gable stole a quick kiss. "Beautiful men deserve beautiful things."

Fuck. That should have been his line. Cutler was older and richer. He could afford to give Gable nice things. Cutler would start with dinner. "Hopefully, tonight makes up for the other night. You should've gotten a proper dinner."

A wicked smile stretched Gable's lips. "I hope you're not apologizing. I might have to leave if you're sorry."

With a shake of his head, Cutler headed for the kitchen. He had to turn away so Gable wouldn't see the way he smiled like an idiot.

Gable spoke behind him as Cutler found a vase for the flowers. "Dinner smells good." Cutler flashed a smile over his shoulder, and Gable continued. "I had a meeting with Saul today."

Cutler fumbled with the flowers, nearly dropping them at the name. Saul had been handpicked by Zander to run his hotels in Atlantic City. As the owner of the Luna name, Zander was extremely particular about who he chose for the role. That closeness also meant Saul knew too much about Cutler. That had always made Cutler uncomfortable. He wanted to walk away from his past and make himself believe he had always been Cutler Maine. He was still a bad person. Cutler lived in Atlantic City for a reason. Just like Saul, he had been handpicked to work the area. It was his job to ensure no trafficking slipped through the Jersey docks. Occasionally, he picked up jobs with the CIA. Every now and then, the CIA and Zander worked together with Cutler. But that was the guy Cutler wanted to be without the shadow of the past. He wanted to forget.

Gable molded against his back, making Cutler realize he had been standing frozen at the counter, lost in a nightmare. His eyes fell closed as Gable's mouth touched his neck. "You don't have a thing to worry about. Saul asked that Case guy to marry him. He's beyond noticing anyone else. This was purely business."

Relief washed over Cutler. Gable thought he had frozen in jealousy. "I met Case on the cruise. He seems nice. Hopefully, Saul won't eat him alive. Was your business fruitful?" The question came out sounding breathless as Gable chose that moment to softly bite his neck. His hands ran up Cutler's chest before gently urging him back, holding him closer. "I'm still alive, so I'd call it a win." Gable didn't sound as if he cared to continue the conversation.

"Will we be skipping a second dinner?"

An evil-sounding laugh vibrated against his skin, sending chill bumps down Cutler's spine. "Maybe I should let you breathe."

Cutler turned. "I could stand to breathe a little less." Again, it was Cutler who went on the attack. Everything about Gable was irresistible. He wanted to watch those tattooed hands move over his nude skin again. Cutler wanted to own him. He very much feared how far he would go. For the first time in a long time, he felt alive. He was scared of what would happen if they stopped. He was equally terrified of what would happen if they didn't.

CHAPTER SEVEN

CUTLER: *IT'S OFFICIAL. YOU'VE ruined dinner for me. Nothing tastes good when you're gone.*

Gable: *When this job is finished and I get back to the hotel, we can FaceTime. You can give me a show and then we'll eat.*

Cutler: *Deal.*

Gable: *Packages arriving at the CIA are thoroughly searched. Now everyone wants to know who sent the good coffee pods and if they can share. LOL!*

Cutler: *I know how much you hate the cheap shit they keep in the break room. It's yours, so you can share if you like. Just not with Roger. That guy tried to stop me from seeing you the other day.*

Gable: *No Roger. Check. I can't wait for this day to end. I miss you like crazy.*

Cutler: *Same.*

Cutler: *Dinner reservation is at seven.*

Gable: *I'll be on time. Promise.*

Cutler: *Hmm. We'll see.*

Gable: *I was late once.*

Cutler: *I'm only playing with you.*

Gable: *If you have to wait, I'll fall at your feet and suck your toes.*

Cutler: **dead* Please don't.*

Gable: *Ahhh. We have a kink shamer.*

Cutler: **hard eye roll**

Gable: *I can make it fun.*

Cutler: *Oh my God. Please stop.*

Gable: *Admit it, you're laughing.*

Cutler: *I'm smiling enthusiastically.*

Gable: *That's good enough for me.*

The restaurant Cutler chose seemed unusually quiet. Of course, that was why he had chosen the place. Its carefully spaced tables, perfect lighting, and general ambiance made it the perfect romantic spot. Cutler showed at five minutes to seven, anticipating a wait. Since Gable often didn't get off work on time, Cutler never knew what time he would show.

"Reservations for Maine," Cutler said as he approached the host.

The man dipped his chin. "This way. Your party has already arrived and is waiting."

Cutler bit back a smile as he followed the small guy through the restaurant to a table near the window. Gable sat, looking relaxed while sipping white wine. He was so fucking sexy. The restaurant had a dress code. Gable fit right in. Cutler loved the way Gable transformed, becoming whatever he needed to be to blend into any situation. Every side of him was gorgeous.

Gable turned his head at Cutler's approach. The smile that lit his face couldn't be faked. A light shone from the inside out. Gable was genuinely happy to see him. Cutler couldn't resist stealing a quick kiss before claiming his seat.

"You beat me here."

Gable laughed. "I had to make up for being late that one time."

Cutler couldn't stop smiling. "I survived it."

For a moment, they simply sat staring at each other while smiling like idiots. Through four months of dating, they had been like this: happy. They never fought. It was just a peaceful coexistence with incredible sex.

Gable set his wine aside and leaned forward. His expression turned serious. "I have something to say."

That didn't sound good. "Okay."

Gable took a breath as if steeling himself. "The last four months with you have been the best of my life. I'm so fucking grateful we met."

The tightness in Cutler's chest got worse. This sounded like a speech gearing up to end them. "But?"

A hint of confusion crossed Gable's features. "There's no but. This has been the best four months of my life."

Relief poured through Cutler. "Same. I had given up on the idea of there being anyone out there for me. You're the best thing that's ever happened to me."

Gable flashed him the sweetest of smiles. "All day, I thought about how best to express myself, because outside of playing the part at work, sometimes I'm not very sure of who I really am. That probably doesn't make sense, but I used to do nothing but work and that became my identity. Then, of course, at work, my identity is whoever they say I am. Sorry, I know I'm rambling. It's just that... damn. What I'm getting at is, I love you."

Cutler blinked. He had gotten carried away trying to keep up with Gable's rapid speech and trying to anticipate where he was headed. Cutler hadn't seen that coming. Gable looked like he held his breath. He released it for half a second to say more. "I know that wasn't very romantic." He immediately went back to holding his breath.

Cutler laughed. He couldn't help it. If he had fantasized about anyone confessing their love to him, that definitely wouldn't have been the speech he pictured. This was better. It wasn't the heat of the moment. This was a thought-out confession. It was perfect. Real. "I love you too."

Gable's chest caved as he released the breath he had apparently still been holding. "You don't have to say it back. I just need you to know how I feel. It's got to be hard dating me. I know I have this job and I'm not always around and—"

Cutler set his hand on Gable's, stopping his nervous chatter. "There's no way you think I'm the type to say I love someone, if I don't mean it. I'm not that nice."

The adorable smile Cutler loved reappeared. "I think you're nice, but no. You wouldn't say it if you didn't mean it."

Again, they held each other's stare in silence. A server appeared, breaking the spell. He set a glass of red wine in front of Cutler.

Cutler's eyebrows snapped together. "I didn't order that."

The waiter smiled. "It's from the gentleman at the bar. He says you're very beautiful."

Gable twisted in his seat. "What the fuck? Am I not sitting right here?"

An older gentleman raised his glass with a smile when Cutler looked his way. "He probably thinks you're my son." Defeat washed over Cutler as the words left his lips. It was likely how everyone saw them.

Gable stood.

Panic soared inside Cutler. Gable had a government job in law enforcement. He couldn't get into a fight.

Gable dug some money from his wallet and tossed it on the table. "Your son, my ass." The grumbled words might have made Cutler smile if he wasn't worried about what Gable might do. Instead of heading the man's way, Gable moved to him. "This just gives me the excuse I need to have you alone. No way in hell will I let anyone think you're anything less than mine." In an obvious show of possessiveness, Gable snagged Cutler's tie, hauled him forward, and kissed him like he would fuck him there if they wouldn't be arrested.

Cutler forgot where they were. A moan rose in his throat.

Gable pulled away. "Let's go. I came by cab so I could leave with you." He looked furious.

Cutler scrambled to his feet.

"Give me your keys."

Cutler handed over his keys while trying to decide if Gable was pissed off at him. He looked angry as hell. Cutler didn't look toward the bar again as he let Gable escort him from the restaurant. He waited until they were safely sequestered inside the car before making a sound.

"Are you—"

Gable was across the car in an instant. His tongue cut off any words Cutler thought he had. Cutler stroked his face. The rough kiss gentled. Pressure and love built in Cutler's chest. He genuinely had never expected to be this happy.

Gable pulled away. He brushed noses with Cutler before swiping another sweet kiss across his lips. "I overreacted. I'm sorry."

"It's okay. I might've done the same."

Gable moved back to his seat. Turned sideways, he held Cutler's stare. "I'm fully aware you're out of my league. That just solidified things. Everyone knows you can do better to the point of me being invisible."

Cutler couldn't have been more shocked if Gable punched him. Of all the things he expected, that wasn't it. "Are you joking? There's no way you actually believe that." Except the hurt in Gable's expression proved it was true.

"You have looks, money, and connections. I'm just some guy with an inconvenient job, so-so credit, and nothing real to offer. The only thing I own free and clear is my bike. You could have anyone. Why would you settle for me?"

"What in the fuck does money have to do with anything?"

"Only someone rich would think money has nothing to do with anything. I literally have nothing to offer someone like you."

A sigh escaped Cutler before he could stop it. "You have love. No one else gives me that. I kill people, Gable. That's who I am. That's where that money comes from. How many people do you think are lining up to love someone like me?" Cutler's throat swelled. Gable had no idea how much hell Cutler had survived. "You're priceless to me." There was no missing the way his voice shook, as if he was on the edge of tears. He might have been humiliated if it was anyone other than Gable sitting across from him. But he needed Gable to understand how much this relationship meant to him. He wasn't ashamed.

For a moment, they simply stared at each other until Gable swiped a shaky hand over his eyes. When it dropped to his lap, he looked defeated. "I'm so fucking sorry. You deserved to know before we started dating that I'm a jealous bastard."

A smile exploded across Cutler's face. "I don't know. That sexy show of dominance was pretty hot."

Gable smiled. It looked guilty. "I feel like a dumbass. I'm not used to having someone matter to me as much as you do."

Gable needed more reassurance than Cutler was managing. "Do you have any idea what I would've done if that drink had been for you?" The accent slipped away as the image of anyone hitting on Gable overcame him. He remembered the way Warren had looked at Gable on that cruise. "No one would see that man again. All because he thought he might have a shot with what's mine. Don't feel dumb. I'm fucking crazy. Just because you haven't seen it doesn't mean I'm stable in any way. I've seen and done things you should hate me for. If anyone tried to take you, you'd be terrified of me." By the time he finished, Cutler shook inside with rage.

Gable's mouth lifted in one corner. "I love you."

The fury bled from Cutler. "I love you too."

"We should get some food to go."

Cutler laughed. "Probably."

Again, they simply held each other's stare. This was love. No one could take it from them.

Steam filled the air. Cutler's mouth on his skin was fucking heaven. Gable hadn't produced a clear thought in an hour. Water assaulted them from every direction. He panted for air while Cutler teased his body. His insides still shook with the fear of losing him. Cutler was here with him. God. He hadn't known he could turn possessive like that. He honestly scared himself a little. When he had turned his head and saw that guy lifting his glass, as if Gable wasn't sitting right there, fuck. He could have killed that guy. Cutler was his.

Gable pushed Cutler against the wall and dropped to his knees. Cutler needed to know no one would make him feel the way Gable did. Before he could suck his prize, Cutler cupped his chin, forcing Gable to meet his stare. His eyes looked haunted.

"I would never want you on your knees for anyone. Not even me."

For the first time, Gable had a bad feeling he had found a PTSD chink in Cutler's armor. The expression he wore nearly broke

Gable. Gable had sucked Cutler dry before. He knew that wasn't the issue. Being on his knees obviously was. Even the way Cutler breathed, as if struggling, showed how bothered he was.

Gable pushed to his feet and killed the water. "There's nothing I wouldn't do for you." He easily swept Cutler from his feet and headed for the bed. The air felt like ice on his wet skin after the heat of the shower. They left a trail of water from the bathroom to Cutler's bed. Gable would worry about that later. For now, he had a man to please.

He crawled into bed and wrapped them in a cocoon of blankets before slithering his way down Cutler's body. Gable wasn't on his knees now. He would get the dick he wanted.

Gable took Cutler down his throat, savoring the sensation of the man's cock sliding across his tongue. Cutler made a sound that had Gable fighting an evil laugh. He knew how to make Cutler fly. A phone chirped. Gable knew it wasn't his. He had left his in the living room. Gable had also turned off his ringer. Cutler was his only priority. The phone chirped again. They ignored the sound. Gable worked double time, bobbing on Cutler's dick. He needed to drink his cum.

The phone chirped a third time. Cutler's muscles tensed. For a moment, Gable thought Cutler meant to check his phone. Irritation ran through him. Then cum filled his mouth, nearly choking him in his surprise. Delicious cries filled the air. Gable's body burned with the need to join Cutler in his bliss.

Cutler pulled his hair, urging Gable higher. Their mouths clashed. His dick ended up in Cutler's skilled hands. He tugged and massaged. Gable's hips rocked, riding the masterful touch. Vaguely, he kept hearing the phone, but he was too far gone to care. He fucked Cutler's palm. Their kiss was almost violent as Gable neared the edge. He needed what Cutler offered. His hips moved faster. Cutler's strokes increased. Gable fought for air through tiny, gasping cries.

"Fuck. Don't stop. Oh, God." Gable made a desperate sound as he soared. The orgasm made his entire body jerk. He couldn't stop crying out against Cutler's lips as Cutler stole his soul. No matter how they made each other blow, it was always beautiful. Gable never wanted to be with anyone else. Their kiss turned sweet as his heart tried slowing to a normal beat. The phone chirped again.

"Oh, for fuck's sake." Cutler snatched up the device. His expression screamed he was ready to tear into someone. His gaze moved across the screen and his expression changed. He looked almost terrifying. "Damn it. Two shipping containers just unexpectedly hit the docks. Thankfully, a worker who keeps an eye out for Zander heard crying coming from inside one. I have to go."

Gable rolled to the side. He was exhausted. "Of course you do. This is important."

Cutler eyed him for a moment, as if trying to decide if Gable was being sarcastic.

Gable tried reassuring him. "I'm serious. You should hurry." He yawned. Fuck. The hot shower, long day, and orgasm had taken it out of him. Cutler stole a kiss and then climbed from the bed. He grabbed a towel and cleaned Gable's skin before tucking him in.

"I'll be back as soon as I can. We'll pick things up then. Until then, get some rest."

Gable didn't need to be told. His eyes were already too heavy to keep open. "Okay. Love you." Even to his ears, he sounded half asleep.

"I love you too." Gable heard the happiness in Cutler's voice. He kissed the tip of Gable's nose. "You won't even know I'm gone."

That was probably true. The darkness already had him drifting.

CHAPTER EIGHT

WITH HIS EYE ON the scope, Cutler scanned the area. He didn't see anything he normally would for jobs like this. There were no extra teams. No illegally docked containers. No guards. He was confused as fuck. When he was certain there was no one to spot him, Cutler rolled upright and dug his phone from his pocket. He scrolled through his contacts until he found Zander's number. It rang twice.

"What's wrong?"

That was a fair way to answer, since Cutler never called. "I'm set up, but there's no one here. There's nothing out of place."

"What are you talking about?"

Cutler's eyebrows snapped together. "What do you mean, what am I talking about? You texted me there was an unexpected shipment and to get to the docks."

"No, I didn't."

He switched Zander to speaker and scrolled through his texts. "What do you mean you didn't? I'm looking at the texts right now." He screenshotted them and sent them to Zander.

"I didn't send those texts. Get out of there." The sudden deadly note to Zander's voice had Cutler's gaze shooting in every direction. He was alone. He had the high ground. There was no way he was currently being targeted. "I don't understand."

"Listen to me, Cutler. Get the fuck out of there. My number has obviously been cloned. Move your ass, now."

Cutler went to work, breaking down his rifle. Still, for reasons he couldn't explain, he argued. "From my vantage, there's no way I'm in danger. I don't understand what the point of driving me out here in the middle..." Realization hit. "I'm not the target. Fuck me, Zander. I'm not the target." He snatched up his shit and ran for the truck.

"Talk to me, Cutler. What's happening?"

Cutler tried to speak through the panic. "Gable. He's asleep in my bed right now."

"I don't know who that is."

Cutler broke every speed limit. Zander's questions gave him something to focus on so he didn't black out in his panic. "Gable. He's the guy I'm dating. From the CIA. He used to work with the contact you sent me to meet in Alabama. Fuck, Zander. He moved here and oh my God."

He heard Zander barking orders in the background. Cutler couldn't focus on anything. "Keep me on the phone. Don't hang up, okay?"

Cutler didn't respond, but he didn't disconnect the call. He was too far gone to worry about anything but the miles between Gable and him. He screeched to a stop outside the garage, unwilling to wait on the slow-ass door to let his truck inside. Cutler stuffed the phone in his back pocket with Zander still on the line. A coldness washed over him as he grabbed a gun from beneath the seat. The door stood open three inches. He strained to hear anything.

"Someone's broken the back lock." Cutler whispered the words, fighting the urge to kick his own ass. He hadn't set the alarm on his way out. That was how certain he had been he would be back soon. Cutler made his way inside, doing his best to listen for any sound and search for any danger while making his way toward the bedroom. The dead silence was almost eerie. It hit him. There was no power. No hum of electricity ran in the background, feeding daily energy vampires. There was nothing but the sound of his pulse beating in his ears.

"Gable!" Cutler shouted, hoping to startle any intruders from their hiding spots. The sound of heavy pants reached his ears. "Gable!"

"I'm here." The whispered words sounded strained.

Cutler flew into the bedroom, ready to get shot as long as he got to Gable. Even in the darkness, Cutler saw the blood. "Oh my, God."

"What's happened?" The muffled voice from his back pocket reminded Cutler he wasn't alone. But Zander was on the opposite side of the country. He couldn't help. "There's blood everywhere." Cutler tried to see the source with no lights. He pulled out his phone and used the flashlight. Gable was in a fetal position. There was too much blood to find the source. Rattling breaths were the only sound he made.

"Holy shit. Hold on, baby. I'm getting help." He didn't hesitate to cut the call with Zander to call nine-one-one. Cutler half-ass heard the call answered. He spoke, panicking as he answered each question thrown his way. It was like no oxygen reached his brain. Blood coated Cutler's hands as he fought to stop bleeding from wounds he didn't understand. He was too far gone to know if Gable had been shot or stabbed or beaten. All he saw was blood that wouldn't stop flowing between his fingers. There was no way someone could lose so much and live. He watched the greatest love of his life slip away from him. Only one thought penetrated his fear. He wouldn't survive this twice.

Blood poured between his fingers. Danilo couldn't die. He had given Cheslav everything to live for in a life so bleak, no one could imagine the horrors. Cheslav had been free. Since just after turning sixteen, he had flown under his father's radar. So much time had passed, he thought his dad had forgotten about him. Cheslav had let himself get complacent. He had let himself fall in love.

He couldn't breathe. Logically, Cheslav knew he was having a panic attack, but it felt worse. It was like his heart would explode any second. He wished it would. No matter how hard he tried to stop the blood from flowing from the dozen stab wounds his father had inflicted, in his heart, Cheslav knew. Danilo was dead. His father sat calmly nearby, covered in the blood spattered from his frenzy. There would be no help called. They were simply waiting for the inevitable. The cruelty rolling from his father in waves was as familiar to Cheslav as breathing. His throat was nearly swollen shut. Hot tears pressed at the backs of his eyes. He felt as helpless and useless as ever.

"You're mine, baby boy. Maybe you'll remember it now."

Cheslav's eyes fell closed. The first tear fell. He had never escaped hell. His dad had just found a new way to torture him.

The scent of antiseptic and despair filled his nostrils. The smell was tinged with copper from Gable's blood covering his hands. He couldn't do this twice in one lifetime. Cutler had truly believed he was free of his father. There could be no doubt this was his doing. Gable's mom's pale hand looked small and out-of-place holding his blood-coated hand. She didn't shy away from her son's dried blood. Nothing mattered but the silent strength they fought to lend each other.

The door to the ER waiting room opened. A man covered from head to toe in tattoos swept into the building like a wraith. People immediately averted their eyes and scurried from his path. Lazarus Melnyk was a face Cutler hadn't seen in years. He hadn't changed much except for a few more tattoos. The guy looked like he belonged in a biker gang. He definitely looked like the executioner he was. There could only be one reason for his arrival. Zander had sent him to kill someone.

His dark gaze landed on Cutler. Cutler held his stare as Lazarus headed his way. He didn't sit. "How's your man?" His voice sounded like he didn't use it often.

"He's in surgery."

His gaze slid toward Gable's mom. He leaned close to Cutler's ear. "I know who did this. Are you in?"

Cutler didn't need to hear more. He stood. "Give me just a second." Cutler met Gable's mom's stare. Her eyes were so much like Gable's, it hurt. They had been in too much shock to share too many words before now. He leaned down and spoke close to her ear. "This is an undercover who works with Gable." It was a total lie, but it was one he knew Gable's mom would believe. She was proud of her special agent son. Plus, her raced flight from Alabama in the middle of the night had her too jet-lagged on top of stressed and scared to question anything. "They've located the man responsible. I have to go. Please text me if you find out anything before I get back."

She grabbed his sleeve before he got away. "I'll keep you posted. Make them pay."

Cutler nodded. He knew she had to see the murder in his eyes. She kissed his cheek and Cutler followed on Lazarus' heels. He was older now and free. This time, he wasn't helpless. Someone had hurt his baby. Hell was coming for them.

It had been years since Lazarus set eyes on Cutler. There was only so much work for people like them. They didn't tend to travel in packs. Plus, they had a different class of client. Cutler had always been polished and charming, having been raised in mafia royalty. Lazarus had come from the dirt. Dirt was what he erased.

It was eerie how quiet Cutler was. Blood coated his hands. He made no move to remedy the situation. It was obvious Cutler was in a dark place. Lazarus wasn't the type to reel in anyone's crazy, but they were walking into hell together. He needed to know Cutler wasn't willing to sacrifice him to get his revenge.

"Your boy works a dangerous job, but he doesn't keep a very low profile."

"I recognize I should've protected him better."

Lazarus fought the urge to snort. "You can't protect him from every enemy he makes in his line of work."

"His work didn't do this. It was my father. I recognize his calling card."

Lazarus scoffed without thinking. He wasn't a compassionate guy, but he realized Cutler was in a bad place. Still, they definitely couldn't rush into what was likely a trap—given how quickly he had gotten the info on Gable's attacker—with Cutler having daddy issues. "Your dad is an eighty-year-old man rotting in prison. His day is long gone. No one would dare cross Zander to strike at you, especially not for him. You were called away for a reason.

This person wanted you out of the way. This wasn't about you. No one likes a snitch and being a CIA agent is a paid snitch. He crossed the wrong one when he chose to drop a bug on Warren Legion, thinking he wouldn't find out who he was. Everyone knows Warren is the right hand of the devil. That's not a dude you play with."

"Sometimes snitches are the only thing standing between a monster and an innocent child." Cutler's words came out sounding deadly, as if spoken between clenched teeth.

Horror overcame Lazarus. He wasn't one to feel guilty, but he hadn't considered his words. Lazarus hated any form of law enforcement. He thought they were useless and more often than not on the take, but he had forgotten Cutler had once testified against his father.

"Look, I didn't—"

"It's fine," Cutler said, cutting him off. "I appreciate you finding the culprit. I had forgotten all about the Warren thing. But it honestly doesn't matter who they are. They're still dead."

Cutler's voice sounded empty and cold. Lazarus got it. Cutler's man had been in surgery for hours. There was a very good chance he wouldn't make it. He couldn't be in two places at once. This needed to be taken care of so Cutler could have quick and brutal vengeance, and he could return to Gable without fear of this happening again.

Their destination came into view. It was a gorgeous house in a secluded area with private beach access. It was the perfect spot for a rich man's right-hand man to live, complete with a watery escape route. They would have to move fast before the guy had time to get away or hide. No doubt the place had a hundred ways to protect its owner, likely including guards of his own. Their window to get to Warren would be small.

It amazed Lazarus that Cutler didn't ask questions as he parked on the street, slightly out of view. He simply slipped from the truck, prepared to go in with nothing but his bare hands as weapons. Lazarus motioned toward the bed of the truck. He pulled back a dark tarp, revealing a cache of weapons. Cutler grabbed a baseball bat, proving he fully intended to make someone suffer for as long as possible.

Every light in the house was on. No alarms sounded or gunshots rang out as they quietly made their way around the property. They circled the house, peering in windows and getting their bearings. It was eerily quiet inside. A man with dark hair sat facing away from the window and toward a TV. That was the only person Lazarus spotted. Nothing made sense other than it being a trap. No way should Warren Legion be this easy to target. They chose the door farthest away from the man, allowing them a buffer from any slight noise picking the lock would create.

Lazarus dug his lock pick from his pocket.

Cutler took a step back and kicked the door in. He was inside before Lazarus had time to recover.

"Goddamn it, Cutler." Lazarus scrambled after him as Cutler stormed into the house. No guards came running. The place stayed silent. No alarm blared. Lazarus knew there was a problem before they made it to the sitting room and to the man they had spotted through the window.

Disappointment ran through Lazarus as he entered the sitting room. A lone man sat upright, completely covered in blood. His dead eyes stared at nothing. A note pinned to his chest with a knife had Lazarus moving closer. He ripped the paper away and read it aloud.

"We're square."

They exchanged a glance.

Cutler eyed a very dead Warren with hatred. "What in the hell is going on here?"

"I don't know." Lazarus read the note again and studied the corpse. "I'm willing to bet half that blood is Gable's. So, who in the fuck killed him? Shit. I was really looking forward to a fight." No one let Lazarus have any fun.

Cutler sighed and pinched the spot between his eyes. Before Lazarus could say more, Cutler jumped and dropped the bat, quickly pulling his phone from his pocket. His eyes moved across the screen. He snatched up the bat and headed for the door, explaining as he went. "Gable made it through surgery."

It seemed priorities had shifted. All Cutler cared about now was Gable. Lazarus was the one left with the itch of an unsolved mystery. He didn't like being in the dark. Cutler might be fine with knowing nothing more than Gable's attacker was dead. Lazarus had to know why. This wasn't over. He had to know more.

Chapter Nine

"I CAN'T BELIEVE YOU bought a new house."

Cutler fluttered around him like a mother hen, trying to get him inside while causing as little pain as possible. "I've always wanted to live on the beach, so this gave me the excuse I needed. There was no way in hell I would let you step a foot back in that old house."

He was so sweet and adorable. "I would've been fine. Honestly, I don't even remember much." Gable winced as he endured the last step from the garage inside the house. A gorgeous kitchen came into view. Everything was blue, and cabinets lined the walls from floor to ceiling. "Oh, wow. You definitely have some storage."

Cutler barely spared a glance for the kitchen. "Some cabinets are actually doors. One is the fridge. Another is a pantry. There's one more that leads to a panic room."

"A panic room? Nice."

Cutler laughed. "Well, some people might call it a storm shelter."

Gable laughed. He immediately regretted it. With a gasp, he grabbed his stomach, trying to keep his insides inside him where they belonged. "Shit."

Cutler somehow managed to look twice as worried. "I'm sorry. I didn't mean to make you laugh."

"Stop apologizing." Cutler hadn't stopped saying he was sorry since the moment Gable opened his eyes in the hospital. "Nothing about this is your fault. I knew my job was dangerous when I took it."

"I should've been there." It also wasn't the first time Cutler had grumbled those words under his breath.

"Oh my gosh. Just help me to the bedroom before I start shaking from being upright too long."

Cutler immediately rushed to help him. "I still say they should've kept you longer."

Gable fought an eye roll. That was a new complaint Cutler hadn't stopped uttering. "Wouldn't you rather I be somewhere where you can take care of me?"

Cutler didn't say anything.

Gable knew he had him. "You can gently cuddle with me here and make sure I have everything I need on our schedule rather than when hospital staff can get around to me."

"That's true."

They came to an open doorway and Gable froze. Not only had Cutler bought a whole new house during the two weeks Gable had been hospitalized, but everything about his bedroom was different. All new furniture and decorative items. Gable's throat swelled. This man really loved him. It wasn't just words.

"You chose a purple duvet? You hate purple."

A sexy chuckle rumbled from Cutler. "It's your favorite color. That's all that matters to me."

Gable shook his head as he eased beneath the covers Cutler turned back for him. "Why would you base all your decisions around me? This is your home. It should be done—shit." Gable panted for breath as he stretched out, making his insides turn to fire. "It should be done how you like." He tried to keep talking and focus on anything other than the pain. "Fuck. I hate this." He rolled to his side and drew his knees up, taking pressure off his wounds. It would take a long time for him to recover from the massive internal trauma. In some ways, he wasn't completely out of the woods. If anything leaked, it could poison his blood. The sepsis would kill him in an ugly and painful way. Gable had always thought of himself as a strong person, but this was beating him. He had never experienced pain like this.

Cutler quickly circled the bed and climbed in next to him. He held Gable, stroking his side and kissing the shell of his ear. "It's okay, baby. I'm right here. Just breathe. If you can last an hour longer, you can have a pain pill."

Gable tried breathing through the pain. "Just hold me and keep talking. I'll be all right. I just need some distraction."

Cutler kept kissing his ear. "You've got it. Anything you want, it's yours. Um, distraction. Okay. I decorated the place for you because I want you to live here. With me. Permanently," Cutler added, as if he worried Gable didn't understand.

He held his breath. Gable didn't know how to react. He loved Cutler, but he hadn't seen this coming. Truthfully, he kind of loved the idea. They were always together, and this was the happiest he had ever been. Plus, his injuries likely meant he would be down for a while and the agency already made noises like this would mean a forced retirement for him. It wasn't personal. He would probably get one hell of a retirement package, but he would be unemployed.

"You don't have to answer right now. I know this was a bad time to ask. Just think about it, okay? Because I don't know if my heart can stand you going back to your place and sleeping without me. I don't know if I'll survive worrying about you through the night. I have some serious PTSD now."

Gable couldn't stop smiling. Fuck, he was in love. "Yeah, I'm not going anywhere. I need you to protect me while I sleep."

He felt Cutler go still. "Did you just agree to move in with me?"

"Yes."

Cutler's lips shaped a huge grin against his neck. "Good."

Gable closed his eyes, still smiling. He could sleep now that the pain had subsided, and he had made Cutler happy. Nothing else mattered. He could survive anything except Cutler hurting. Gable just needed some rest. His body was exhausted.

For way longer than necessary, Cutler listened to Gable breathe. It was such a calming sound that soothed Cutler's frayed nerves. Since Gable came out of surgery, Cutler's entire focus had been on making Gable's life easier and better. He didn't have time to think about the people behind this. The man who hurt him was dead. It seemed the entire incident had the CIA in an uproar, so whoever ordered the attack hadn't done themselves any favors. Staying under the radar was a criminal's first line of defense. So this had been a dumb as hell move. It was one Cutler wouldn't imitate. Gable had survived. Cutler would tighten their security, batten down the hatches, and keep sentinel. He knew now there was an enemy out there. Cutler was smart enough to protect his and let bigger fish eat his prey. Considering Lazarus kept hanging around, Cutler had a feeling he was on the job. Gable had his full attention.

Even in his sleep, Gable still shook slightly. He knew it was a combination of trauma, blood loss, and pain. Cutler wanted to spend the rest of his life making him better. He would start with handling Gable's things, getting him moved in and settled. Cutler had to keep his mind busy. He hadn't been joking about the PTSD. Cutler hadn't even returned to the scene. He had paid a company to handle the old house and the mess. Every time he closed his eyes, he saw a mixture of Danilo and Gable bleeding to death in his arms. His heart was beat up and tired. Cutler kept it to himself, but sometimes the past drowned him. There was so much ugliness in his mind and heart. All Cutler wanted was a peaceful life.

Cutler sniffed. His eyes burned and his throat swelled. He just wanted to hold Gable like this for the rest of his life and leave everything else behind. He sniffed again. The air stuttered from his lungs.

A loud cry escaped Gable, shattering Cutler's heart as Gable rolled. His baby shook harder as he buried his face against Cutler's throat. "Shh. It's okay. I'm not going anywhere."

Until Gable hurt himself trying to comfort Cutler, he didn't realize he silently cried.

Life had just been too overwhelming. "I'm fine. Go back to sleep."

Gable held him tighter. "I'll never be too hurt or tired to hold you. You go to sleep too. Don't act like I don't know you've been staying awake all night, keeping me safe with the hospital's lax security. Close your eyes."

Cutler did as told.

"Take a breath."

Cutler breathed.

"Relax. I need you to be my pillow."

A soft chuckle escaped Cutler. Gable shouldn't be comforting him, but it was just another sign of how perfect they were together. He settled in to be the pillow Gable needed. His warmth soothed Cutler's soul. In no time, Gable's even breathing had the darkness coming for Cutler. Everything would be fine.

CHAPTER TEN

GABLE COULD SAY WITHOUT an ounce of hesitation that Saul and Case's wedding was the most extravagant thing he had ever witnessed. Every detail was over the top, from the flowers to the food. The couple looked happy. That was Gable's biggest takeaway. He had never seen two people smile as hard. Alcohol flowed freely. The elite danced with anyone and everyone except their spouses. It was quite the show. Gable wasn't up to drinking and partying just yet. He enjoyed watching, though. Exhaustion still kept his feet still.

A bored-looking young buck in an overly expensive suit appeared at Gable's side while he waited for Cutler to finish a conversation with some men Gable had never seen. They had their heads together, looking like they plotted something Gable didn't want to know. Still, he couldn't take his eyes off the man who had stolen his soul.

"So, Saul is officially off the list of Atlantic City's most eligible bachelors. When are you pulling Cutler off the list?"

Gable looked the guy's way. He looked like a bored, rich daddy's boy who had never been told no. His brown hair was perfect, and his eyes looked dead.

When Gable didn't respond, the guy's cold gaze moved from where Cutler stood to meet Gable's stare. "Apologies. Noir."

It took Gable a second to realize the guy meant Noir was his name. He pasted on a patient smile. "Gable."

"I know." He sipped his champagne. "So, when can we expect your wedding announcement?"

Gable opened his mouth and then snapped his teeth together. He had no idea how to answer that.

Cutler appeared at his side. His arm encircled Gable's waist. "What are you talking about?"

Gable fought a blush.

Noir looked unmoved. His voice stayed as bland as if he spoke about the weather. "Marriage. I asked when Gable intends to take you off the market."

A good-natured laugh escaped Cutler. "I haven't been on the market since the day I met Gable. He's ruined me for anyone else."

"Pity." Noir walked away without a backward glance.

Gable fought the usual surge of jealousy. People cared not at all they were a couple. He wanted to be proud of having such a sexy and obviously sought after man, but mostly people's dismissal of him left him frustrated.

Cutler kissed his ear. "Dance with me."

Since it was a slow song and Gable needed the reassurance of Cutler holding him publicly, he took Cutler's hand and headed for the dance floor. Cutler held him close and moved extra slow, as if scared of exhausting him. His chest eased each second that passed. Cutler always chose him. In fact, he acted as if there were no other options. His shoulders relaxed.

The scent of Cutler's cologne called to him. He buried his nose in the crook of Cutler's neck and inhaled. Peace and love washed over him. He was always at home in Cutler's arms.

"He's right. I should take you off the market."

Cutler's arms tightened around him. "I wasn't humoring him. There's zero hope for anyone else. You're it for me."

A hint of nervousness set in. It was honestly something he had been thinking about for a bit. "I'm being serious. We should do it."

Cutler leaned away enough to meet Gable's stare. "Do what?"

"Get married." Gable wouldn't shy away from what his heart wanted. They already lived together.

"Okay." Cutler simply went back to holding him closely, as if he hadn't just accepted a marriage proposal.

Gable wanted to slap himself. "I'm sorry."

Cutler leaned away again. He looked upset. "Don't take it back."

"Oh, I'm not." Cutler wasn't getting away from him now. "I'm sorry I did one more thing as unromantically as possible. You deserved a beautiful proposal with a ring and wine or music or whatever."

A line appeared between Cutler's eyebrows. "There is music."

Gable sighed. Sometimes, it was pointless to try to explain things to Cutler. He simply didn't understand how inferior he felt sometimes in comparison. Then Gable always ended up doing things like this that showed even more how lacking he was.

Cutler buried his face against Gable's neck. "I have you in my arms," he breathed against Gable's throat. "We're dancing at a wedding where two people stupidly in love just got married. There's so much love in the air, it's cloying. This is romantic." Gable wasn't convinced, but he was willing to let it go. He told himself he would make it up to Cutler when he bought a ring. Then Cutler continued, making Gable's throat swell. "Sometimes, I don't think you really understand the life I had before I created this one. I can say I lived in the deepest hell, but there's no way you can know what you don't know. There was no loving home or protection. There was just this twisted man who savored every new torture he conceived. You can't know. I'm glad you don't." He kissed Gable's neck. "But that also means you don't understand how much this moment means to me, or how I feel every day when I wake up next to you. I see you and I know genuine love. You just told me you want to give me that love forever." His arms tightened around Gable, as if scared Gable would disappear. "You can't know."

He was right. Cutler was so amazing. Sometimes, Gable forgot that Cutler had chosen to be this amazing man. He had been tortured by an evil man. Those years could have twisted him into a mirror image. He hadn't let that happen. That was exactly why he deserved everything.

"I love you."

"I love you too."

Gable ran his hands up Cutler's back. "Can we go home? I'm a little tired."

Cutler didn't hesitate to take his hand and head for the exit. Gable wanted to save what was left of his energy for his baby. His heart needed to show him love.

It had only been two months since Gable had been released from the hospital. His extensive injuries would likely take several more months to heal. Gable still had very little energy. Cutler had worried the wedding would be too much, but Gable had wanted to go. Leaving without as much as a goodbye mattered not at all to Cutler. All he cared about was Gable's health.

In their bedroom, he helped Gable undress and get ready for bed. He looked exhausted. The angry red scars from the dozens of stab wounds he had endured broke Cutler's heart every time he saw them. He hated the way Gable's gaze always shied away under Cutler's stare when they were visible. Nothing could take away his beauty in Cutler's eyes. He kissed a scar near Gable's collarbone.

Gable sucked in a ragged-sounding breath. They hadn't made love since the night of his attack. Gable's body couldn't endure it. Cutler didn't care if they never had sex again as long as he had Gable's love. But he would be lying if he said he didn't crave him. His body stirred, just being this close to his nudity.

"You should take off your clothes too."

Cutler chuckled. "I'm not so sure that's a good idea at the moment. Your sexy body is tempting me too much tonight."

"Good."

Cutler went still. He couldn't let Gable get hurt for him. "I—"

Gable cupped his erection through his pants and stroked. "Take off your clothes, Cutler." He hesitated. "Unless you don't want me anymore now that I look like this." He sounded as if he truly feared that was the case.

Cutler's hands immediately went to work on the buttons on his shirt. Gable helped by working on Cutler's pants. They weren't frantic. More methodical. They had a goal. "Tell me how not to hurt you." Cutler didn't care how badly they wanted this. He wouldn't let Gable set back his progress.

"Trust me."

With a nod, Cutler followed Gable's lead. They kissed. The sweet way their tongues brushed had love swelling in his chest. He never got enough. They touched and kissed their way to Gable straddling him in bed. Gable's erection felt heavy against his cock. Cutler was hyperaware of every place their bodies touched. Before Gable, Cutler had gone years without being touched. Now a couple of months without Gable's body against his like this felt like forever. He was weak.

Cutler watched as Gable sat back on his heels and eyed Cutler's body. His eyes were full of love and lust. Beautiful. Gable stroked Cutler's torso. "Every inch of you turns me on."

"Same." Cutler heard the breathlessness in his voice. He was too aroused to make his throat work properly. But he was also calling on every ounce of his willpower because Gable had to be the one who chose every move. Cutler wouldn't risk hurting him for any amount of pleasure.

Gable reached for the bedside table and found the lube. While straddling Cutler's thighs, he oiled Cutler's erection. "Part of me wants a huge wedding. I want everyone to see how crazy we are about each other—like Saul and Case did. Another part of me doesn't want to wait." He kept his gaze locked on his hands, stroking Cutler while he spoke. "These past few months have made me realize how short life is and how quickly everything can be ripped away." His gaze lifted and collided with Cutler's stare. He looked devastated. "I don't want to die not being your husband."

Cutler's throat swelled. "I'll never let that happen."

Gable shifted positions and slowly lowered himself onto Cutler's cock. Cutler shook with need as Gable's tight body stretched around his dick. He wondered if he would go insane. Gable's heated expression was enough to have Cutler ready to blow.

"Fuck. You're so sexy. Sitting on my dick, you're immaculate." The Russian accent he fought hard to keep under wraps couldn't be hidden. Gable was too far in his head.

The slow way Gable moved had Cutler's brain ready to snap. Still, he stayed motionless, allowing Gable to choose what he could handle. Gable's eyes closed and his nostrils flared as he gently rocked himself on Cutler's cock. Cutler ground his back teeth so hard, he worried they would turn to dust. It had been too long since Gable's heat engulfed him. He badly wanted to grab Gable's waist and slam himself over and over again inside the tight asshole he loved.

In no time, Gable's breathing turned ragged. The pressure climbing Cutler's cock threatened to blow just from watching Gable use him for pleasure.

"Goddamn. I wish you could see how turned on you look. You have me hanging on by a thread. You're too sexy."

Gable's lips parted. His cheeks flushed. Cutler nearly popped a blood vessel fighting not to come. Then Gable's gorgeous green eyes focused on Cutler, boldly holding his stare as a gasp fell from his lips. His body tried sucking Cutler deeper as cum hit Cutler's chest. Cutler's will snapped. He reached up and found the underside of the headboard. Cutler gripped it so hard, he worried the wood might crack. He fought to not lift his hips and fuck his way through Gable's orgasm. Instead, he let Gable's body gently milk him. When his orgasm hit, he swore he lost the ability to see. He heard his own cries and couldn't stop. The muscles in his thighs felt like they might snap from the rigid way he held himself, forcing himself not to move while Gable took care of him, pleasuring him. He had never been as close to insanity as he was in that moment. His entire body shook from the blinding pleasure.

Then Gable was settled in his arms, and their tongues entwined. Nothing existed but their love. He would marry Gable immediately. They would still have the big wedding, but later. Gable deserved that. But the marriage couldn't wait. Gable was right. Everything could disappear tomorrow, but they would go as one. This was his soulmate. He had to make that official.

Chapter Eleven

With Cutler's delicious body draped over him like a blanket, Gable toyed with Cutler's wedding ring. Several times, he felt a smile touch Cutler's lips against his neck. He hadn't known there was this much happiness in the world until Cutler gave it to him by marrying him. Gable didn't speak because he had too much to say that words couldn't express. He had married his best friend, the greatest love of his life, and the knowledge overwhelmed him every day. Gable didn't miss his job the way he expected. Everything had changed since falling for Cutler. He didn't regret a damn thing.

Cutler's phone chirped. A loud groan vibrated against his neck. "Why? Why does this always happen when we're cuddling?"

Gable shook with laughter. "To be fair, we're always cuddling."

Cutler stretched for the phone while Gable enjoyed the show. He never tired of savoring Cutler's nudity. "I'm getting too old for this shit."

Gable's gaze slid down Cutler's tight body. "You don't look too old to me."

Cutler shot him a wry look, making Gable laugh harder.

"Where are we headed?" Gable asked, trying to drag Cutler's thoughts away from his age. Since his attack, Cutler had refused to leave Gable alone while he worked. He had threatened to quit until Gable agreed to accompany him as a spotter. It gave Gable something to do and Cutler peace of mind. Gable couldn't live with knowing they both had stopped doing what they could to make the world a safer place. It genuinely wasn't that big of a change for him. Nights of hiding, playing at reconnaissance, took him back to his days as a SEAL. As his hand ran down Cutler's bare hip, he wondered if Cutler was right, though. Maybe they were getting too old. The bed felt too good. Cutler's body draping his made him lazy. He seriously considered quitting everything except this.

"False alarm. It's your mom sending me a recipe she saw on Facebook."

A bark of laughter burst from Gable. "I swear she never sleeps, and she loves you more than me."

Cutler settled back down, keeping Gable warm. "Nah. She loves me because of how much she loves you." He kissed Gable's neck. "Thank you."

"For what?"

He felt Cutler shrug. "For sharing her with me. I never had a mom. I never had anyone before you."

God, it broke Gable's heart when Cutler said things like that. "You never have to thank me for loving you. It's the easiest thing I've ever done." He kissed Cutler's forehead. "Mom feels the same."

The attention Cutler paid to his neck turned from sweet to toe-curling. Gable's breathing changed. He heard the shift. Cutler obviously did too. "Let me know if you're tired of me."

"Never." Goddamn, even to his ears, he sounded like a thirsty whore. He gave no fucks. Every moment with Cutler was like a dream. He planned to savor every single second until there was no breath left in him. This was his person. His husband. His soulmate. He wouldn't trade Cutler for anything. Not the return of his job or to go back to the zero-pain living he had before his attack. Gable was ruined for anyone else. That was fine. This was all he needed.

Keep an eye out for the next Atlantic City's Most Wanted, *Demented*.

About the Author

CHARITY PARKERSON IS AN award-winning and multi-published author with several companies. Born with no filter from her brain to her mouth, she decided to take this odd quirk and insert it in her characters. One of her greatest loves is writing morally gray characters. You'll find them scattered throughout her hundreds of titles.

*Eight-time Readers' Favorite Award Winner

*2015 Passionate Plume Award Finalist

*2013 Reviewers' Choice Award Winner

*2012 ARRA Finalist for Favorite Paranormal Romance

*Five-time winner of The Mistress of the Darkpath

Connect with her online:

*Sign up for her newsletter: https://bit.ly/charityparkersonnewsletter

*Join her readers' group on Facebook: http://bit.ly/CharitysTribe

*Website: https://www.charityparkerson.com

*A list of her social media accounts and giveaways all in one place: http://hy.page/charityparkerson

www.ingramcontent.com/pod-product-compliance
Lightning Source LLC
Chambersburg PA
CBHW060352180626
46817CB00008B/2986